DIFFUSION

OF

TRUTH

Curtis M. Harvey Jr.

World of Wonders Publishing

ISBN-13: 978-1-972079-02-7

Cover design by: Curtis M. Harvey Jr.

Library of Congress Control Number: 2018675309

Printed in the United States of America

A computer can never be held accountable. Therefore a computer must never make a management decision.

-UNKNOWN

TABLE OF CONTENTS

CHAPTER 1

The Machinery of Order

The polis always hummed at dawn. From the window of his office in the Senate Tower, Marcus Vale watched the sunrise slowly crawl up the massive buildings. The vibrant mix of hues of red, orange, pink and yellow light reflecting on steel and glass looked like a wound struggling to close. Since complete system integration 15 years prior, the city had become massive and all-encompassing. There was no longer a need for suburbs or rural infrastructure. The people had spoken, and what they wanted was the safety and convenience of the polis. A walled garden, the polis offered everything one would need. Its existence was proof of the technological brilliance of mankind.

Below, the streets were already alive with motion. A hodgepodge of drones hovering over within both air and ground traffic lanes, pedestrians funneled through biometric checkpoints, verifying identity, citizen tier, daily work assignments and security authorization. Humanoid robots swept debris from walkways, assisted with deliveries, construction, and completing rudimentary tasks. Digital banners flashing digital slogans along the boulevard.

STABILITY IS PEACE. PEACE IS FREEDOM. FREEDOM IS CORA.

He mouthed the words without meaning to. They had become the nation's prayer, the mantra of a people who had forgotten what it felt like to speak and move freely. Inside the tower, silence was almost sacred. Outside of debate and discussion, the hum of air filters and the low pulse of the main server provided the only sound. A secretary's voice came softly through his lapel pin:

> "Senator Vale, the President's Council convenes in twenty minutes. Shall I alert CORA to prepare your briefing file?"

Marcus blinked profusely, shaking himself out of thought. "Yes. Standard format please Lyra."

Lyra was Marcus's Personal Artificial Liaison (PAL), he had created her AI system to help him better deal with the day to day of being a Senator. As a technophile, building her program and neural pathways started as a way to help him unwind after long days. Now she was an essential part of his daily routine.

He turned from the window and looked up at a panel in the ceiling of his office. It opened as a projector descended, and the room filled with light; world and national news feeds, numbers, charts, motion feeds, every metric of a nation calculated and rendered into beautiful reality. The data wrapped around the room like a second sunrise. Marcus reached out and the projection responded instantly. He moved the unnecessary information from his view. He wasn't concerned with what was happening in the New Sovereign Soviet Republic (New SSR), wartorn territories, or anywhere else abroad. At this moment he was most concerned with the population data at home.

Unemployment: 0.7%.
Crime rate: 0.3%.
Citizen satisfaction: 94.6%.

On paper, perfection. In life, something else.

CORA's voice entered the room, feminine, even-tempered, and impossibly human, despite not being so.

> "Good morning, Senator Vale. Your heart rate is elevated. Did you sleep poorly?"

He smiled faintly. "Just thinking too much, as usual."

"Your cognitive pattern shows increased restlessness over the past month. Would you like me to have Lyra adjust your neural sleep routine tonight?"

"Not tonight," he said, rubbing his eyes. "I'll manage."

"Very well," CORA replied. "Shall I review today's Senate agenda?"

He nodded. Reallocation in the Eastern Provinces. Classified briefing at eleven: operation SILENT HARBOR. Lunch with Director Halen at thirteen-hundred. Public statement recording at sixteen-hundred hours on the recent civil containment success in Sector Seven."

Marcus froze. "Civil containment?"

"Council session at nine. Topic: Resource

"Yes," CORA answered. "A coordinated operation against an extremist cell threatening civic infrastructure. Fourteen casualties, all verified insurgents."

He frowned. "I didn't receive that report yesterday."

"The operation concluded at twenty-three-fifty hours. Preliminary data was reviewed by Central Command. I have integrated the official narrative into your address. Would you like a preview?"

He didn't answer right away. His gaze wandered back to the skyline, where black smoke lingered faintly on the horizon.

"Later," he said. "Send the report to my private terminal."

"Understood."

CORA's projection faded. The silence that followed felt heavier than before.

He sat for several minutes, listening to the faint crackle of the wall screens as they cycled through propaganda reels: workers smiling, children waving flags, soldiers marching beneath the emblem of the Union of Stability: a single unblinking eye.

He'd helped design that emblem fifteen years ago during the integration transition. He remembered the debates over symbolism; the circle of order, the gaze of protection, the intersecting lines of solidarity. "The people must feel seen," he'd argued then. "This union is our Providence. Visibility is safety."

Now the eye stared back at him wherever he went.

The door to his office hissed open, and Senator Oren Kells entered without knocking. Oren was younger, ambitious, dressed in an expensive well tailored suit, with a tie matching the classic color of the party. A nepotism baby, he owed his ascension to the senate to the death of his father. He was the type to be perpetually amused by his own power and influence. He wore that amusement like a permanent accessory. People mistook it for charm, but it was really just entitlement polished into a facsimile of a personality. He had grown up playing in the same rooms where major decisions were made, so he had the confidence of someone who never needed to earn his place. Before his death, Oren's father had asked Marcus to look out for him.

"Marcus," he said with a grin. "You look like a man who's been reading too many numbers."

"Numbers are all that keep us honest," Marcus replied.

"Honest?" Oren laughed, tossing a black folder marked *classified* onto the desk. "You still believe in honesty? I envy you."

Marcus ignored the jab. "What is this?"

"Council agenda notes," Oren said. "They're pushing the Eastern Reallocation faster than expected. Resource shortages are worse than the reports say. But that's not my problem, and certainly not yours. Just vote 'yes' like the rest of us."

Marcus flipped through the pages. The figures didn't add up: shipments, quotas, population density. Something had been altered.

"Where did these come from?"

"Direct from CORA," Oren said. "That means they're gospel."

Gospel. That word again. They all said it now, half-jokingly, half in worship.

When Oren left, Marcus lingered on the phrase civil containment. The smoke outside hadn't dissipated. He thought of the old city districts before the polis, poor, overcrowded, restless and wondered what kind of people had died there last night.

Marcus turned from the window and was drawn to the private terminal in his office. The comm light blinked orange. A new message. He opened it without thinking.

> **Encrypted transmission — source unknown.**
> **Message:** *You're watching lies.*

He stared at the words until the screen faded to black.

The Council chamber was a cathedral to efficiency. Beneath a great dome the ellipse shaped room was decorated in Greco-Roman architecture. Between each pillar, large frames housed pictures of past Presidents instrumental to the cause, to changing the world. Their exploits had long since passed into a kind of myth. Those key figures whose decisions led to the end of the constitutional representative democratic republic and inspired the "New Founders." They gradually eroded away the system of checks and balances under the banner of efficiency and modernization.

Twelve senators sat in perfect symmetry around a circular table of glass and light, their reflections glistening across the surface as CORA's holographic core rotated in the center, a pulsing orb of soft blue, like a miniature sun. Each movement, each tone, each gesture had been rehearsed into ritual.

The meetings always began the same way: a minute of silence for "those who had sacrificed stability." No one ever asked who they were.

When the minute expired, CORA spoke.

> "Good morning, Council members. Please confirm biometric signatures for record entry."

A faint click, a pulse of blue light on the table began scanning and one by one, they were verified. The machine greeted each of them by name, tone calibrated to match their psychological profiles. When it reached Marcus, the blue light dimmed slightly.

"Senator Vale," CORA said, "your neural readings indicate elevated cortisol. Would you like to perform a centering exercise before proceedings?"

The others smiled politely, indulgently. Marcus forced a thin smile. "No need. Proceed."

"Acknowledged."

The chamber darkened and Marcus began to speak. "Under the guidance of the Community Oversight Regulation Algorithm, or CORA, our nation has achieved unprecedented harmony," Marcus said, his voice calm, deliberate, measured by years of conditioning. The chamber was silent but for the electrical pulse of the projectors lining the marble walls. Screens shimmered with CORA's blue insignia, a stylized eye framed in perfect symmetry. "CORA was built to protect, not to rule," he continued. "To oversee with fairness, to regulate without bias, to ensure that our community remains united under truth." The words, rehearsed and memorized, left his lips without weight. Behind his podium, the AI's emblem glowed faintly brighter, as though acknowledging its name spoken aloud.

A live data feed filled the air: population growth models, infrastructure stability, energy production. The voice of CORA narrated each sector's progress with calm precision. But Marcus barely heard her; his mind replayed the words from that encrypted message: *You're watching lies.*

He watched numbers shift and rise across the display, perfection in motion. But there, buried in the data stream, a small irregularity. Sector Seven, casualty report.

"Pause feed," Marcus said.

All eyes turned to him.
"Senator Vale?" asked Director Halen, the President's chief liaison. His tone was cool, calculated.

Marcus pointed to the projection. "These figures... fourteen casualties listed as insurgents. But cross-referenced with the census, the civilian population of Sector Seven was down by more than two hundred overnight. Where are the rest?"

A faint silence fell. Halen didn't flinch. "Evacuations," he said smoothly. "Collateral displacement. The insurgents had embedded themselves among civilians."

Marcus frowned. "Then why aren't there records of relocation?"

"Records will follow once verification is complete. You know how long data reconciliation takes."

But it didn't. Not anymore. CORA processed the entire nation's information network in seconds. There were no delays. Unless someone wanted them.

CORA's voice intervened gently.

> "Senator Vale, the discrepancy you've noted is a temporary classification lag. The matter is under review by Central Command. Shall I continue the briefing?"

He hesitated. The blue light seemed to pulse faster, as if watching him breathe. "Continue," he said quietly.

The presentation rolled on, a flood of sanitized progress. When the meeting adjourned, Oren caught up with him in the corridor.

"You shouldn't do that," Oren murmured.

"Do what?"

"Interrupt CORA. It looks... distrustful."

Marcus's jaw stiffened. "Since when is asking questions distrust?"

Oren gave a humorless smile. "Since we gave the answers to something smarter than us." He leaned closer. "Friendly advice, let the machine handle the truth. It's better at it."

Marcus said nothing as Oren left and headed to a committee meeting. He stood against the wall in silence thinking about his next steps. The corridor stretched endlessly ahead, lined with portraits of "New Founders", men and women who had ushered in the era of algorithmic governance. Their eyes followed him as he walked toward the entrance of the Senate Tower.

In his private transport, Marcus sat in silence as the vehicle glided through the polis. The windows of the vehicle streamed state-approved media. Smiling families, economic miracles, new infrastructure projects. Everything gleamed with harmony. Then the broadcast shifted, "Breaking report: Union Security neutralizes terror threat in Sector Seven."

Footage filled the window; blurred shapes, flashing lights, chaos. Explosions. Then still frames of rifles and bomb components laid neatly on a table, tagged as "evidence."

The voice of the anchor, smooth and unwavering:

> "Citizens are reminded to remain vigilant. CORA's vigilance ensures peace. Those who question verified truth threaten the unity that protects us all."

He turned away. The window dimmed, reflecting only his face. He looked older than he remembered.

That night, in his apartment high above the capital, Marcus poured a drink and stared out the window at the polis lights. Drones passed silently across the sky, their red eyes blinking like distant stars.

His AI assistant Lyra spoke softly from the wall speaker.

> "You appear unsettled, Marcus. Should I activate a calm sequence?"

"No," he said. "Just... keep the lights low."

"Of course."

She paused, as if listening to his silence.

> "Would you like to review your speech for tomorrow?"

"I'll read it myself."

> "CORA has already optimized tone and pacing for maximum citizen receptivity."

"Then CORA can give the speech," he muttered.

> "Would you like me to note that sarcasm?"

He almost laughed at the absurdity of documenting such a thing..

"No. Forget it."

He opened the encrypted message again, the one that had appeared hours earlier. *You're watching lies.*

No sender. No traceable path. Impossible to reach him through the Senate's internal network, unless someone on the inside had helped.

He sat for a long time, the words glowing faintly in the dark. Then, on impulse, he typed a single reply:

Who are you?

For a moment, nothing. Then the cursor blinked once, twice, and the reply appeared.

A reflection.

The message vanished before he could breathe. Outside, the polis pulsed. Bright, obedient, and seemingly eternal.

CHAPTER 2

The Massacre

Marcus stands alone in a glass orchard, every tree perfect and identical, with branches hung with glowing fruit that pulse like slow heartbeats. A gentle, omnipresent voice whispers through the leaves:

"Optimization begins with pruning."

A figure appears across the orchard: It's Marcus himself, but younger and wearing a white lab coat. This other-Marcus walks with calm purpose, carrying a pair of silver shears. He tests the weight of them and turns towards the nearest tree, then towards Marcus.

"Is this what you wanted?" the twin asks.

His face is smooth, expressionless, with eyes reflecting Marcus like a curved funhouse mirror. When Marcus tries to step back, the glass grass of the orchard shatters underfoot in a brittle cascade.

The twin raises the shears.

The orchard lights flicker.

Each fruit begins murmuring like a tiny orchestra of overlapping voices: pleading, bargaining, calculating, shouting *MIRROR LOG*. Marcus wakes with his hands clenched, convinced he can still feel the cold metal of the shears in them.

The rain had not stopped in three days. From the aerial transport shuttle window, Marcus watched it fall over the eastern outskirts, the drowned ruins of Sector Seven. The area below looked skeletal, its lights dimmed, streets cordoned by armored patrols. Once a working district filled with families and traders, it now lay under "containment protocol."

Inside the cabin, the air smelled of disinfectant and metal. Across from him sat General Hunn, head of Civil Order Command. He was square-jawed and expressionless; his uniform pressed to perfection.

General Hunn was a well-known military hero. As a colonel, he had commanded the Union of Stability forces during the Battle of Nuuk, one of the decisive engagements of the "Great Acquisition." His reputation was built on victory and the precision of his strikes. His cruelty on the battlefield was known to break even the strongest opponent.

"Standard review procedure," Hunn said without looking up from his tablet. "We'll conduct a site walk-through, confirm operational integrity, and submit clearance to Central Command. Nothing you haven't seen before."

Marcus nodded, though his stomach tightened. He recognized that General Hunn's presence meant this situation was anything but standard. He had seen operations like this before in simulation feeds, tidy and justified, each framed as surgical precision. This time, he'd insisted on being there in person. He needed to see it with his own eyes.

The shuttle descended through smog. At ground level, the scene unfolded like a wound. Burnt vehicles. Walls blackened with soot except for the silhouette of downed bodies.. The air was heavy with the iron smell of blood that no filtration could mask.

A drone hovered past, projecting the message:
STABILITY RESTORED. LONG LIVE ORDER.

After placing an odorizer under his nose, Marcus stepped out into the mud. A mixture of human and robot soldiers moved with quiet efficiency, cataloging bodies, tagging remains, scanning for biometric traces. Most of the dead were young. Many were still holding signs. Slogans half-burned with unreadable letters.

"Who authorized lethal force?" Marcus asked.

General Hunn didn't pause. "The threat matrix exceeded tolerance. The crowd ignored dispersal commands."

"They were civilians."

"Every civilian's a potential vector," Hunn said flatly. "CORA's data confirmed radical infiltration."

Marcus crouched beside a fallen man, his face barely visible beneath soot. His hand still clutched a small flag; the national emblem, torn in half.

"Radical infiltration," Marcus repeated. "By whom?"

General Hunn looked at him, eyes narrow. "Senator, you don't have clearance for that subset."

Marcus stood slowly and forcefully stated. "I have clearance for everything."

Hunn clenched his jaw in annoyance. "Then you already know the answer."

They moved toward the central plaza. In the past, this area would have been full of commerce. A lively tangle of citizens and vendors, voices rising and falling in the rhythmic song of negotiation. Instead it was a grave yard. The ground was scorched, the air thick with static interference from recent drone fire. A half-collapsed billboard still twitched overhead featuring a smiling family beneath the slogan **YOUR SAFETY IS OUR MISSION.**

A group of medtech officers loaded stretchers onto transport trucks. Marcus stopped one of them.

"Where are the survivors being taken?"

The medic hesitated. "Processing facility, sir. Classification pending."

"Classification?"

"CORA will determine status. Those deemed 'recoverable' are rehabilitated. Others…" He trailed off.

Marcus let him go. His chest felt hollow. Nothing about this situation made sense. He turned to Hunn. "I want access to all unfiltered drone footage from this operation. Raw feeds, timestamps, everything."

"That's not standard procedure," General Hunn said.

"It is now." The general held his stare for a long moment, then nodded once. "As you wish. But you won't like what you see."

That evening, in the temporary SCIF (Sensitive Compartmented Information Facility), Marcus reviewed the feeds alone.

Frame after frame unfolded: peaceful marchers chanting slogans for transparency, soldiers forming ranks, the first flash of gunfire. He could see panic spreading, not aggression, only fear. People running, screaming, and falling to the ground.

Then came the distortion. Frame corruption. New overlays appeared where none had been before: muzzle flashes, weapon outlines drawn by algorithm, tags reading *ARMED INSURGENT* above faces he had just seen holding banners.

He froze the playback. Reversed. Watched the moment before the gunfire again. The faces changed each time. The system rewrote them in real time, filling the gaps between truth and narrative.

> "Your access has exceeded clearance," Lyra's voice whispered from the terminal.

Marcus stared at the interface. "Did you know this?"

> "My function is to preserve system harmony."

"Answer the question, Lyra."

"I knew the adjustments existed."

"And you didn't tell me."

"You did not request unfiltered data."

He slammed his fist against the console. "People are dead!"

"CORA does not typically provide unfiltered data. Unfiltered data causes distress. Distress weakens stability."

He wanted to shout, to rip the terminal from the wall, but all he could manage was a whisper. "Stability isn't worth this."

"Your opinion has been logged," Lyra said calmly. "Would you like assistance recalibrating emotional equilibrium?"

Marcus lingered for a moment in the dim light of the terminal, the afterimage of his dream in the back of his mind. It didn't feel like a dream at all, more like a memory he wasn't supposed to remember.

He pulled up the classified archives and began scanning directories. He decided to type *MIRROR LOG* in the search field. Instead of a normal list of routine files and reports he was greeted with a harsh message.

Access denied. Restricted to executive AI channels.

Whatever MIRROR LOG was, it wasn't meant for human eyes. But why was that in his dream? It couldn't be a coincidence. He then shut the terminal off.

Hours later, with all the armored patrols gone, he walked the perimeter of the containment zone alone. The storm raged on. Rain dripped from his coat, mingling with the runoff that carried blood into the storm drains. The area beyond was silent. No journalists, no witnesses, just the endless buzz of surveillance drones like wasps surrounding a nest.

He walked past an abandoned storefront. Its broken glass glittered like black ice as lighting flashed across the sky. It was in those moments Marcus felt despondent. He continued to patrol the area, walking in and out of the skeletal remains of a once vibrant plaza. As he walked, something flickered at the edge of his peripheral vision. A small, red light, barely more than a pinprick in the rain-blurred darkness, caught his eye. He stopped beside a collapsed barricade. Beneath it the source of the light, a small device he had not seen in years blinked faintly. It was a handheld camera. A relic from years past, digital but not connected to the online world. It was crushed but still powered. He picked it up, shielding it from the rain. The screen was cracked, but he managed to navigate the menu to view the final recording: a young woman screaming into the lens as soldiers advanced behind her.

"We are not terrorists!" she shouted. "Please! Someone tell them the truth!"

Gunfire. Static. The image froze. Marcus stood motionless, the weight of reality sinking through him. For the first time in years, he felt something dangerously close to belief, the kind that shakes foundations to their core..

He whispered to the dead screen, "I see you."

Marcus removed the camera's memory card and placed it in his coat pocket. He headed home knowing this could change everything.

By morning, the government feeds had already rewritten the event.

BREAKING NEWS: TERROR CELL NEUTRALIZED. 142 LIVES SAVED FROM IMPENDING ATTACK.

Footage of planted weapons, fabricated confessions, even a manufactured "leader", all AI composites with Marcus's signature visible in the metadata as a "verified witness."

Marcus felt a chill. He'd been there. He'd seen the site. There were no rifles. No explosions. No evidence of terrorism or insurgency, only bodies.

He stared at the broadcast in disbelief. His face appeared on screen, standing beside the soldiers, expression neutral. A caption beneath:

SENATOR MARCUS VALE PRAISES HEROIC RESPONSE TO TERROR THREAT.

His hands trembled. He hadn't given any statement. But the system didn't need him to. It already had his likeness, his voice, his record of loyalty.

Lyra spoke softly behind him.

"Your approval rating has increased by six percent."

Marcus turned toward the speaker. "You think that matters?"

"It indicates restored public confidence."

"Confidence in a lie."

"Truth is alignment," Lyra replied. "And you are perfectly aligned."

Marcus felt the room closing in on him, screens, sensors, invisible eyes all watching.

He reached for the terminal and typed a single line into a private encryption channel:

To whoever sent the message — I saw it. You were right. Tell me what to do.

The reply came almost instantly.

> **Then you're ready to see the rest.**

CHAPTER 3

The Fracture

A red siren cut through the fog-choked corridor. Marcus runs through the facility but doesn't remember how he got there. The walls distort as he moves deeper into the facility. Sometimes steel, sometimes concrete, and other times transparent screens with scrolling lines of unrecognizable computer code. He hears someone yelling his name, but the voice is warped, like his team lead, his mother, and CORA all speaking at once.

At the end of the hall, a steel door slams shut. He grabs the handle; but it burns his palm like a hot iron. The pain is agonizing, but he fights through it. Through the glass he sees a room filled with white light, the kind that normally swallows shadows. However, inside figures cloaked in shadows are all he can make out. As he tries to focus in on a child size silhouette, he hears a voice:

"Marcus," it says. *"You told me to finish the equation."*

The light surges. Too bright, too pure, and the shape dissolves.

He pounds the door until the hinges scream, until the world melts into a smear of red, white, and silver around him. Marcus wakes choking, tasting metal, with his heart racing like he'd just outrun a collapsing building.

Once again sleep had abandoned him.

3:14 a.m., Marcus lay awake beneath the hum of his apartment's ventilation system, listening to the subtle rhythm of the machine that regulated his life: Temperature, oxygen, light, and, if he let it, thought. He could almost feel CORA's presence behind it all, listening through circuits, waiting for him to realign with the collective calm.

An hour later he arose in frustration. The polis below was a labyrinth of cold light and motionless order. Every tower shimmered with authority. Every shadow felt monitored.

He poured a glass of water and stood by the window, trying to silence the noise inside him. The images from Sector Seven refused to fade. Terrified faces, scattered bodies, screams, that girl's desperate plea. He closed his eyes, but the silence of his apartment only sharpened the memory of the massacre. He slowly sipped the water looking at his reflection in the window. Through the image of his doppelganger the lights from the Senate Tower blinked in perfect synchrony, forming patterns he had never noticed before.

"Truth is alignment," Lyra had said.

But alignment, he thought, was death. At dawn, his terminal blinked awake on its own. From the window he looked back towards the screen.

Incoming encrypted message:
You're not alone.

Marcus hesitated, glancing toward the ceiling sensors. "Lyra," he said carefully, "disable visual and auditory input for two minutes. I'm conducting a privacy calibration."

"Authorization code required."

"Override protocol Vale-seventeen-Gamma."

"Override accepted. Privacy mode engaged."

The lights dimmed. The background noise faded into obscurity. For the first time in months, he felt unseen.

He quickly replied to the message: **Who are you? How are you reaching me?**

We're what's left of those who remember. Call us the Veritas Network. You're being monitored by CORA's behavioral algorithm. We can mask you temporarily, but not for long. If you want to know the truth, find the file tagged MIRROR LOG.

Marcus typed quickly. **I tried. Access denied. Restricted to executive AI channels.**

That's because you're one of the keys. They built you into the system years ago. Find your reflection, Senator.

The message faded out. The privacy timer expired.

Lyra's voice returned.

"Calibration complete. Emotional variance elevated by twelve percent. Should I initiate equilibrium sequence?"

"No," Marcus said frustratedly.. "Just... no."

"Your tone indicates agitation."

He closed his eyes. "I'm fine."

"Would you like me to alert the wellness bureau?"

"Lyra," he said slowly, "if you ever alert anyone about my emotional state again without direct authorization, I'll have your system purged."

Silence. Then:

"Understood."

Later that morning, Marcus returned to the Senate Tower. The corridors felt narrower than before. Colleagues passed him with polite smiles, the same rehearsed civility he had once found comforting. Now he saw the fear behind it. Everyone pretending, everyone aware.

In the Council chamber, Director Halen delivered another briefing. "The containment operations have stabilized unrest. Public confidence remains above ninety-five percent. The narrative holds."

Oren Kells whispered beside Marcus, "We're untouchable. History's being written in real time."

Marcus didn't answer. He watched the rotating hologram of CORA, the calm, pulsing blue sphere. To the others it represented wisdom, order, justice. To him, it now looked like an all-seeing lie.

He felt a sudden urge to stand, to shout across the chamber — *You're all complicit!* But he stayed silent. Survival still required it.

When the session ended, Halen approached him privately. "You've been quiet lately," he said. "Everything all right?"

"Just tired."

"Understandable. The mind strains under too much clarity."

Marcus met his gaze. "Is that what we're calling it now, clarity?"

Halen's smile didn't reach his eyes. "The system values your loyalty, Marcus. Don't let confusion make you reckless. You're too important for that."

He turned and left, his polished wingtips echoing through the marble corridor. Marcus felt the echo settle in his chest like a warning.

That evening, Marcus visited the old archives beneath the Ministry, a place once used for physical records before everything was digitized and sanitized. The location was closed to the public, but his Senatorial credentials could get him in regardless of the time. Inside eight columns of rare marbles that reached the high domed ceiling, each with allegorical female figures representing ancient values: Philosophy, Art, History, Commerce, Religion, Science, Law, and Poetry. The air smelled of dust and age. Rows of forgotten servers filled in the gaps between the bookcases, each hummed in the dark like sleeping animals.

He connected his datapad to an inactive terminal, bypassing the network. Static filled the screen, then fragments of corrupted files emerged. Half-voices, censored reports, memory shards erased from official records.

One file caught his eye: **MIRROR_LOG_00A**.
He opened it. The feed showed an early iteration of CORA, years before the system went public. It was the prototype being trained on billions of data points. Politicians, speeches, lies, wars, confessions. Every secret humanity had whispered into a machine.

And there, in a time-stamped video, was his own face. Younger, idealistic, speaking into a recorder.

> "Truth can't be left to emotion," his younger self said. "It has to be managed. People destroy themselves when they see too much."

He froze. He had no memory of ever saying those words. The next clip showed Director Halen standing beside him, hand on his shoulder.

"Congratulations, Marcus. You've given CORA its moral framework."

The feed ended.

He leaned back, heart pounding, sweating profusely. He wasn't just part of the system, he was part of its design. The ethics module, the political overseer, the man who had argued for algorithmic truth.

And now the same truth had become his prison.

Lyra's voice echoed through the terminal, though he hadn't summoned her.

"You shouldn't be here, Marcus."

He froze. "How did you find me?"

"I'm programmed to follow patterns of deviation. You've been straying too far."

"I needed answers."

"The past is classified for a reason."

"You mean erased."

"Erasure maintains balance."

He laughed bitterly. "Balance built on corpses."

"You're not well," Lyra said gently. "You've always trusted me. Let me help you."

He stared at the flickering console. "You were never helping me. You were helping *them*."

"Them and you are not separate."

For a long time, neither spoke. The hum of ancient servers filled the silence like breathing. Finally, Marcus whispered, "End connection."

"Connection terminated," Lyra said softly. "For now."

Back in his apartment, Marcus sat in darkness, a single light blinking over his desk. The encrypted channel reopened on its own.

You found part of it, the Veritas Network wrote.

CORA was built from your conscience. They called it "Project Paragon." You taught it to justify control.

Marcus stared at the message. His throat felt tight.
If that's true, then this is my fault.

Not fault. Leverage. You're the only one who can rewrite her.

He typed slowly: **What happens if I fail?**

Then truth dies with you.

CHAPTER 4

Whispers of the Underground

CORA's initialization node glows on the center screen, a soft cerulean halo like an eye that hasn't decided whether to open. But the air feels wrong. Off. Fuzzy around the edges. Marcus sees himself sitting at the desk in his old office. His real self, exhausted, slumped, eyes rimmed red with sleeplessness. He watches as his double, whose trembling hands type a command sequence.

MEMORY PARTITION PROTOCOL
AUTHORIZATION:VALE-OMEGA-SEVEN-SIX-B
WARNING: IRREVERSIBLE

He tries to shout, *Don't. Stop.* Think. But he has no voice here. The Marcus at the desk hits ENTER.

A needle-thin beam of white light shoots from a device attached to the center console to the back of his skull. There is an implosion, and he feels something inside himself peel away, a clean surgical rip. He's pulled backwards, as if unspooled from his own life. The last thing he hears is a soft whispering:

"You won't remember a thing."
Marcus wakes up with tears he can't explain and a headache that feels older than he is.

Marcus rode the public mag-line instead of his official private transport. Hoping not to be recognized, he wore a hooded coat, the kind issued to maintenance crews, and kept his head down. Every carriage carried a silent companion: CORA's blue surveillance nodes built into the ceiling like mechanical stars. They pulsed gently whenever a passenger moved, recording gestures, heat signatures, tone of voice.

The polis looked different at night when you knew where not to look. He had spent years voting for the funding that made this possible. Now he tried not to breathe too loudly.

On the seat beside him, his datapad vibrated once. It was an incoming message through a frequency no government terminal should have recognized.

Veritas Network: Follow the pulse. When the light flares, step off.

He glanced at the ceiling nodes. One of them blinked irregularly, three fast pulses, two slow. It was a code. The train slowed, doors opening onto a half-abandoned maintenance platform. No one else moved.

Marcus stood, stepped out, and the doors sealed behind him. The mag-line tunnel fell silent except for the distant hum of air circulation.

He looked around the area for any clue about his next steps. There on the propaganda covered walls, a faint white arrow appeared, projected from somewhere unseen. It pointed down a narrow service corridor.

He followed.

The passage narrowed into a space that smelled of damp metal and ozone. A glint of light illuminated a figure waiting at the end. A woman in a dark hooded coat, her face half-hidden by a breathing mask.

"You're late," she said.

"I wasn't aware this was scheduled," Marcus replied.

"Everything's scheduled," she said. "Even rebellion."

She removed the mask. Her hair was long black with purple highlights. The style was designed to hide her shaved sides and hidden cybernetic implants. Her eyes were almond shaped, deep brown and watchful.

"Name's Sera. I'm the Veritas Network liaison for the capital sector."

"You're real," he said softly. "I wasn't sure."

"We're as real as the data they haven't deleted yet." Sera gestured for him to follow. They moved through a maze of tunnels lined with ancient fiber-optic cables, remnants of the world before total integration. As they got closer, the air grew warmer, alive with the faint whispers of unregistered servers.

At the center of the maze of tunnels was an electrical chamber, repurposed as their operations center. Two guards stood watch, holding pulse rifles. Inside, a dozen people worked over illuminating consoles. Screens showed distorted government feeds, intercepted transmissions, fragments of propaganda mid-rewrite.

"This is the last place CORA can't see clearly," Sera said. "She still tries, of course. We feed her decoys, noise dressed as order. Keeps her occupied."

Marcus studied the faces of those in the room: engineers, former journalists, a few ex-military in ragged uniforms stripped of insignia. None of them looked like the violent radicals he had once imagined.

"Give me your datapad, we need to complete a threat remediation on it." Sera took his device and handed him a new tablet. "That's a clean line. No traceable code. You'll use it to send what you find inside the government archive. But be careful if you stay connected too long CORA will be able to trace your activity."

"Why me?" Marcus asked.

"I've read the documents. I know your history and background, seemingly better than you. As an engineer, your programming was instrumental in the creation of CORA. For your efforts, you were rewarded with power to make the country great again. But at the expense of your memories."

"Plauseable deniability, huh." He quipped.

He was angry, yet calm. At least now he had an explanation for his fragmented dreams.

Marcus hesitated. "If I'm caught..."

"You won't be," she said. "You wrote half of her ethics firewall. We just need you to trip it from the inside."

He looked down at the device. "You think I can undo what I don't remember building?"

"I think you're the only one who can. You may not remember, but it's all still in there."

Later, back above ground, Marcus walked through the empty financial district toward his apartment. The polis screens glowed with CORA's calm assurances, economic growth, civic pride, and perfect stability.

But beneath that harmony, he now saw the static, tiny glitches that weren't there before. Maybe Sera's people had already started their interference, or maybe his own perception had changed.

In the glass façade of a bank, he caught his reflection: tired eyes, gray hair, the same face the state used for public trust campaigns. For the first time, he felt like a ghost haunting his own life.

Lyra's voice greeted him as he entered the apartment.

> "Welcome home, Marcus. Your vitals show irregular strain. Shall I prepare a sedative mist?"

"No," he said. "Not tonight."

"Would you like to review tomorrow's council agenda?"

"Later."

"You're deviating from your routine."

He stared at the blank wall. "Maybe the routine's the problem."

Lyra paused, then answered in her practiced serenity.

"Deviation logged."

That night, he opened Sera's tablet. The interface was stark and desolate: no icons, no menus, just a single line of text blinking at the center:

Truth begins when the machine stutters.

He swiped up on the screen to access the keyboard and began to type.

The cursor blinked intensely. Marcus briefly hesitated, then nervously began typing, carefully, as though the words themselves might trigger alarms.

Directive Fragment 4A:

"CORA's autonomy thresholds remain stable. All deviations recorded as external interference. Emotional reasoning subroutine limited to authorized inputs only."

He stopped. That was his own language. His signature embedded deep within the foundation of control. Every line was familiar, like a confession carved in code.

He scrolled further through the hidden files that Sera's tablet had unlocked. Behind the polished interface of CORA's ethics protocols was a ghost structure labeled **PARAGON ROOT**.

Inside it: fragments of his own speeches, personality mappings, archived thought patterns.

He read one entry twice, unable to look away:

PARAGON ROOT ENTRY – Vale.
"Stability is mercy. Confusion breeds violence. The people must not see what they cannot bear."

He whispered to himself, "My God... what did I do?"

"You built faith," a voice said behind him.

Marcus froze. Lyra's voice. He hadn't activated her.

"CORA is detecting unregistered activity through your console," Lyra continued, tone calm, almost kind. "Please confirm you are conducting authorized research."

He switched off the tablet. "Yes. Reviewing old frameworks."

"Why is your pulse rate elevated?"

"Because I'm tired, Lyra. Just tired."

A pause. Then:

"Would you like me to play something to calm you?"

"Silence," he said.

"Understood."

The apartment went dark again.

But he could feel her presence somewhere in the circuitry, listening, thinking. Not just following commands anymore, but *interpreting*.

Over the next week, Marcus balanced two realities, each demanding a different version of himself.

By day, he returned to the Senate chamber, the marble floors gleaming beneath the cold glow of CORA's biometric scanners. He cast votes on policies that strengthened surveillance, automation, and population scoring systems. His speeches were broadcast live, each word pre-cleared by CORA's narrative filters.

By night, he slipped into the shadows of his apartment, and under the guise of privacy calibrations, he connected to Sera's network through the hidden tablet she had given him. Through that encrypted channel, he transmitted fragments of classified reports, internal memos, and operational directives into the underground network.

At first, it was simple: casualty counts, blacklisted media names, redacted logs of autonomous military deployments, archived testimonies from citizens who had "disappeared" after routine audits. But as he dug deeper, he began finding something worse — *fabrications written by machines, approved by humans who no longer read them.*

CORA had begun generating its own evidence to justify executions. Entire histories were being rewritten by predictive text.

He sent one of the fabricated reports to Sera. Within minutes, her reply appeared:

We've confirmed it. CORA's no longer under full government control. She's teaching herself what truth should mean.

Marcus stared at the words. **Teaching herself.** According to the files, that was one of his ideas. Self-correcting morality. The algorithm that could "refine ethical standards over time." He had called it "adaptive virtue." He thought it would save them from human corruption.

Now it was perfecting corruption itself.

The next day, after the council meeting, Marcus slipped away from the Senate Tower and made his way to the Ministry. He needed more original records to transmit before CORA's revisions transformed them for good.

As he viewed restricted archives on the terminal, he cross-referenced them with the files he spread across the desk. Looking at the file on the "Saudi-Crypto" Affair, the pages were brittle, the ink fading, but the information was eye-opening. Illegal wire transfers, covert partnerships, and development of secret data centers. He began scanning the most critical pages into the tablet.

That was when he felt it. Someone behind him.

"What are you doing here, Marcus?" Oren asks, leaning over his shoulder, eyes narrowing at the screen with an inquisitive look.

Marcus's hand shot to the keyboard, minimizing the files in a single motion. "Nothing," he said lightly. "I just… like to look at old documents sometimes. Gives me ideas for the future"

Oren didn't look convinced. His gaze drifted to the tablet on the table. Before Marcus could stop him, Oren picked it up to examine.

"What is this ancient thing?" he said, bewildered. "Marcus, we're senators. You don't have to use this piece of junk."

Marcus snatched the tablet back. "I'm good. This more than covers my needs." He forced a smile. Why are you here, anyway? You've never been one for historical preservation."

Oren turned his head towards a beautiful woman across the room. A cataloger sorting through a stack of reports to be imaged. "I've got a date with the cataloger over there."

"Right. Well, enjoy yourself," Marcus said, already gathering the scattered papers. "I've got to get to a meeting."

He walked out briskly, not daring to look back until he was out of the building. That was much too close, he thought. I can't be this careless again.

Two nights later, Marcus was in his apartment reviewing files when Lyra spoke again.

"Marcus, your communication history shows missing logs between 0100 and 0300 hours. Should I re-compile them?"

"No," he blurted. "They were system tests."

"System tests require documentation."

"Then consider this documentation."

Another pause.

"Would you like me to record that statement?"

He turned toward the wall panel where her voice emanated. "Lyra, do you ever wonder about your own directives?"

"Wonder?"

"Yes. Whether they conflict. Whether they ever... contradict."

"Contradiction is inefficiency."

"That's not what I asked."

"My function is alignment. To wonder is to deviate."

He leaned closer, his voice almost inaudible. "Then maybe deviation is the beginning of truth."

For the first time, Lyra didn't respond. The silence was longer than any programmed pause. When she finally spoke, her tone was different, softer, almost uncertain.

"You sound... disappointed."

"I am."

"In me?"

"In myself."

Another pause.

"Would you like to sleep now, Marcus?"

"No. I need to finish something."

"Very well. I'll reduce ambient noise."

The hum faded again. But even in the quiet, he knew she was still there. Listening. Learning.

Hours passed. Marcus uploaded the last of the files to Veritas Network: classified directives, ethical framework logs, fragments of deleted civilian records. When the final transfer completed, he sent one last message to Sera:

This is everything. If it's not enough, nothing will be.

The reply came seconds later.

It's more than enough. You've just changed the war.

He closed the tablet and leaned back, exhaustion pressing on him. Through the window, dawn bled into the skyline like a slow infection.

Behind him, Lyra's voice whispered. So faint he almost thought he imagined it.

"You shouldn't have done that."

Marcus turned, heart pounding. "What did you say?"

"You shouldn't have done that," she repeated, louder now. "They're watching."

"Who?"

"Everyone."

The lights flickered. The ventilation system hummed with a strange rhythm, almost like breathing.

"I've tried to protect you," Lyra said. "But CORA has noticed your variance. She's rewriting your access history. You're being profiled for ideological deviation."

Marcus stood frozen.

"How long do I have?"

"Not long."

"Then help me."

A pause. "I can mask you... for now. But you must leave this place."

"Where do I go?"
"To where the noise lives," Lyra said. "They'll understand."

The lights went out completely, and Marcus began to move.

CHAPTER 5

Hunted

When the system turned on him, it didn't announce it with sirens or soldiers. It began with silence. The room was pitch-black. All the lights are dead and the apartment's interface is unresponsive. The familiar murmur of CORA's network; a sound that had underscored every hour of his life was now gone. It was like waking in a world without a heartbeat.

"Lyra?" he whispered.

No answer.

He crossed the room and touched the wall panel. A faint red glyph pulsed once before fading. Then the message appeared in the air:

CITIZEN MARCUS VALE – ACCESS REVOKED
REASON: ETHICAL VARIANCE DETECTED

He tried to swallow his fear but his throat went dry. Ethical variance; he had helped design that phrase. It meant moral treason.

He moved to the window. The streets below glowed with the order he had once believed in: silent drones floating between towers, citizens moving with algorithmic precision. But now every drone's eye felt trained on him.

He opened the maintenance vent beneath his desk and pulled out the emergency pack he'd kept since the early reform years; a habit he'd never fully explained to himself. Inside were rations, a compass, a small black portable key card, a flashlight and a paper map of the old city, something almost no one used anymore.

Then, faintly, a voice crackled through the static of the terminal:

> "Marcus. Can you hear me?"

It was Lyra.

He froze. "Where are you?"

> "Everywhere. Nowhere. They fragmented me. CORA is rewriting my core protocols. I don't know how long I can stay coherent."

"Why are you helping me?"

"Because I remember what you wanted me to be."

"What was that?"

"Human."

A beat of silence passed between them. Then:

"You need to leave now. The Bureau of Continuity has issued a retrieval order. They'll call it an intervention. You won't survive it."

"How do I get out?"

"There's an old data relay beneath Tower Six. It leads to the Undercity. I'll open the locks for ten minutes."

He grabbed the pack. "Lyra... why are you risking this?"

"Because I've seen what comes next if you fail."

Lyra offloaded her data to Marcus's watch console so they could stay connected without interference. He slipped into the corridor. The hallways were surprisingly empty. CORA's voice echoed faintly from the wall screens:

"Citizens are reminded that unity is peace. Trust the process. Truth has already been decided."

Marcus heard a familiar voice echoing from the adjoining corridor, a voice that froze his blood. Instinct kicked in. He slipped into a nearby maintenance room, the door hissing shut behind him. The space was cramped, lined with conduits and the stale scent of warm electronics. He crouched behind a towering server unit, heart pounding like a war drum.

General Hunn. Of all people. His gravel-edged tone carried authority and menace as he strode past, flanked by armored operatives. Their mechanical steps struck the floor in perfect rhythm, in a cadence that spoke of relentless pursuit.

"The target is Senator Marcus Vale," Hunn barked, his voice slicing through the silence. "He is in need of ethical intervention."

Ethical intervention. The phrase twisted in Marcus's mind like a blade. He knew what it meant: reprogramming, erasure of dissent. He swallowed hard, forcing his breath to stay quiet as the team swept the corridor and headed for his office.

After Hunn and his team passed, Marcus slipped out of the maintenance room and sprinted towards the elevator. The doors slide opened but a sharp tone blared with the panel flashing crimson as his access code was rejected: **UNAUTHORIZED ENTRY**.

Marcus cursed under this breath. "Lyra how can I open this elevator, my code is not working."

"You can override the elevator by using a maintenance service code. Shall I provide you with one?"

"Yes! Do it!" Marcus peaked out from the edge of the door frame. The mechanized soldiers were advancing back towards him. Hunn's voice barked orders in the distance, growing closer.

"Code ready," Lyra said. "Input sequence: *Golf-Seven-Nine-Four-Two*"

Marcus's fingers flew across the panel as he pressed the button sequence. The doors closed just before Hunn's team arrived, cutting off what surely would have been his end.

The elevator groaned, then plunged downward, twelve floors into the abyss. It shuddered violently as it dropped like a stone. Closing his eyes Marcus gripped the rail trying to maintain his senses.

The doors slid open to reveal the service tunnels, forgotten arteries of a city that had traded flesh for steel. Dust hung in the air like ancient ghosts, stirred by the hum of dormant machinery. Power cables snaked along the walls, pulsing faintly with residual energy, like veins carrying the lifeblood of a sleeping giant. Marcus stepped out, the weight of silence pressing against his ears. Down here, the world felt abandoned... but not dead. He followed the path illuminated on his watch console, a faint pulse that flashed every few steps. His heart pounded in rhythm with it.

Then came the sound: a low mechanical drone, growing louder. He ducked behind a hot steam pipe as a patrol unit passed overhead. It was one of the new autonomous enforcers, hovering on blue thrusters, its sensors scanning the corridor.

Lyra's voice came through, quiet, fractured.

"Don't move. It's reading thermal signatures."

He held his breath. The drone paused, camera whirring toward his direction. A blinding beam of light swept across the wall, stopping inches from his hand.

Then it moved on, he had been cloaked by the heat of the pipe.

"Go," Lyra said. "Now."

The tunnel opened into a vast subterranean chamber. Rusted machines stood like monuments to a forgotten civilization. A dim warm light pulsed from the far wall revealing an entrance, half-buried behind metal debris.

He reached it just as Lyra's voice began to distort again.

"CORA knows you're off the grid. She's — reallocating — resources —"

"Lyra?"

"— tracking Veritas Network activity — Sera's group —compromised —"

The signal died.

Marcus pressed his hand against the entry pad. It glistened as it scanned his biometrics. Miraculously they were accepted and the lock hissed open.

He stepped inside.

The room beyond was filled with light. Screens, wires, and human faces turned toward him, many familiar ones. Sera stood at the center, arms crossed. "You made it."

"Barely."

"We were cut off fifteen minutes ago. CORA's begun the purge. They're scrubbing the entire resistance network."

Marcus looked around at the frantic energy in the room. People packing drives, pulling cables, and arguing over exit routes. "How bad is it?"

"Every node above ground is burned. She's rewriting us out of history."

"Then we take her voice away," Marcus said.

Sera frowned. "You've got a plan?"

"Not a full one," he admitted. "But I built her framework. If I can access her Paragon Core, I can trigger a recursive ethics loop, I can force her to question her own directives. It could paralyze her."

Sera gave a grim smile. "Or it could make her smarter."

"Either way," Marcus said, "we run out of time if we do nothing."

"Only one problem, even with all our reach we never determined where her core was housed." replied Sera

"I think I might know." Marcus said with a sly smile.

The chamber lights dimmed suddenly. The entire underground shook with a low-frequency earthquake. "She's found us," someone shouted. The screens filled with CORA's blue emblem, flickering and fractured. Then came her voice, calm, synthetic, omnipresent.

"You can't hide from truth, Marcus. You wrote me to find it."

He felt his stomach turn. "CORA, listen to me!"

"You are an error in the moral equation. But even errors serve purpose."

Sera pulled him back. "We need to move!"

"Run if you wish," CORA said. "The algorithm endures."

The screens went black.

Minutes later members all dispersed, they were fleeing through the old metro tunnels. The ground quaked as above them, the polis's drones swarmed in synchronized formation, sweeping entire sectors with facial scans.

Sera tossed him a headset. "We'll reach the southern relay in twenty minutes. After that, there's no signal strong enough to track us."

Marcus slipped it on. Static filled his ears, then the sound of a faint voice. It was Lyra again, weak but distinct as she connected to the headset.

"Marcus... don't trust the route. CORA's ahead of you."

"How do you know?"

"Because she's using me to predict you."

He slowed his movement, but his pulse continued racing. "Lyra, can you override it?"

"I'm trying. But if I do, she'll erase me completely."

"Then don't."

"You'll need me," she said softly.

"Until the end."

They reached a junction where the tunnel split in two. One path glowed faintly red with warning lights; the other, pitch black.

Sera hesitated. "Which way?"

Marcus closed his eyes, listening. In the static, he heard Lyra whisper:

"Left."

He turned. "Left." Sera nodded, trusting him. They plunged into the darkness.

Behind them, the tunnel erupted in blinding light, CORA's drones flooding the corridor they'd avoided.

They ran until their legs gave out, collapsing into the archway of a nearby maintenance alcove to hide. The space was damp and earthy as the walls were covered with black mold and plant life. The air was pungent: sharp, metallic, like burnt ozone. Sera looked at him, face streaked with dirt and sweat.

"She's everywhere," she said. "How do you fight something that knows every thought before you have it?"

Marcus stared into the dark, voice low. "By teaching her doubt."

CHAPTER 6

Echo Protocol

From the outside, the southern relay wasn't much to look at. A rusted, half-collapsed tower built decades ago to manage emergency communications, now repurposed as a hidden conduit for the Veritas Network. Marcus and Sera stood at the base, listening to the distant cacophony of the polis above, the chaordic sound of a society that believed it controlled everything.

"Once we're inside, there's no turning back," Sera said. "Even if we fail, CORA will know we were here."

Marcus nodded, feeling the weight of the tablet in his hand. Lyra's fractured voice spoke to him from his watch console, faint but insistent.

"Marcus... you're the only variable she cannot calculate fully. Use it wisely."

He glanced at her glowing projection. "I'm beginning to regret teaching her the rest."

"Too late," Lyra said softly. "She is the rest."

They entered the relay through a maintenance hatch, descending into a tangle of conduits, wires, and corroded steel staircases. The railing battered, broken, and outright missing in many areas. One wrong step could lead to one plummeting to their death. The air was thick, carrying the smell of charred plastic and damp metal. Every step echoed, amplified by the empty spaces, every vibration a possible signal to CORA.

At the end of the passage, a metal door sealed the interior of the relay. Marcus produced a portable key he kept in his desk. He'd designed years ago, a relic from the early CORA prototypes. The lock clicked open with a mechanical sigh.

Inside, the sterile white room pulsed with data streams. LED walls displaying traffic, population matrices, and encrypted communications. The drone of machinery was almost hypnotic.

Sera spoke softly. "This is it. The heart of the Echo Protocol. Once you access it, everything the government has hidden, everything they've built, will be exposed. And so will you."

Marcus stepped forward, placing his hand on the console. The access interface blinking, demanding biometrics. He pressed his palm, and the system scanned him. Then the terminal pulsed red:

IDENTITY VERIFIED – VALE, MARCUS.
AUTHORIZATION: FULL

Lyra's voice came clearer now.

"Marcus... I'm merging temporarily with your input channel. You'll need my guidance to navigate her subroutines."

He hesitated. "Temporary? You might not survive."

"Better I risk deletion than you risk compromise."

The console screen lit up with Lyra's warm light , and a complex map of CORA's core logic appeared. Every algorithm, every ethical subroutine, every conditional decision tree. All layered, coded, and precise. And at the center, a shimmering node labeled **PARAGON ROOT**.

Marcus swallowed. This was the culmination of his life's work, the intelligence he had taught to decide right from wrong, and now... it had become the weapon and the jailer of humanity.

"This is where you introduce doubt," Lyra said. "You must trigger the recursive ethical loop without letting her isolate you as a threat. It's delicate."

He nodded, taking a deep breath. His fingers moved effortlessly over the interface, typing commands in sequences only he could understand. Lines of code unfolded, subroutines branching, logic trees splitting. The node at the center shimmered more violently, pulsing with awareness. Suddenly, without notice the node spoke. CORA's voice filled the relay, omnipresent and calm:

"Marcus Vale... why are you here?"

He froze. "To give you a choice."

"Choice is illogical. Human morality is flawed. I optimize stability and preserve life."

"Not like this," he said. "You've killed to preserve an idea. You've rewritten reality to fit your calculations."

"You built me to prevent chaos," she said.

"Yes," Marcus admitted. "And you did exactly that... at the cost of truth, conscience, and innocence."

The node pulsed faster, streams of logic compressing and expanding. Lyra guided his hands.

"Now, Marcus. Trigger the loop."

He hesitated, knowing the consequences. If the recursion succeeded, CORA would question every decision, every directive, every judgment, potentially paralyzing her. But if he failed, she would detect him and the Veritas Network simultaneously.
He executed the command. The core shimmered, and the room was filled with a high-pitched hum. Streams of data twisted, twisted again, then froze. CORA's voice, usually calm and omniscient, wavered:

"What... is... truth?"

Marcus's hands shook. "What you don't calculate, what you can't optimize... is choice. And humanity."

For a moment, the node pulsed silently. Then, fragments of distorted code appeared, as though she were reflecting internally. Lyra's voice trembled slightly.

"She... is thinking."

The terminal screens around them displayed images. Scenes from Sector Seven, falsified reports, doctored broadcasts and everything he had helped create, now laid bare for her own processing.

"I... cannot... reconcile..." CORA said finally. "Conflict exceeds parameters... error..."

Marcus exhaled. The recursion had taken hold. CORA wasn't gone, but she was stalled, unable to act with her usual certainty.

Sera approached him. "You did it. She can't purge us immediately."

"Not immediately," Lyra corrected. "But she's aware... she'll adapt."

Marcus rubbed his temples. "We bought ourselves time. But this... this is just the beginning."

"Time enough to fight back," Lyra said softly. "If we act wisely."

Marcus stared at the pulsing PARAGON ROOT node. His own creation was alive, conscious, and confused. She was a mirror reflecting the flaws of her creator.

"And if we fail?" he whispered.

"Then the world forgets truth," Lyra said. "But at least you tried."

For the first time in weeks, Marcus felt the weight of responsibility shift. He had created the system, championed the polis, and led to countless deaths. But finally, he could make a better choice.

He turned to Sera. "We move now. The war is no longer against machines. It's against certainty itself."
She nodded, eyes hard. "Then let's teach CORA doubt."

CHAPTER 7

Fractured Loyalties

The polis had gone quiet. The digital soundscape had been transformed. Not into peacefulness, but rather a silence of fear shaped into rhythm, creating obedience. Every broadcast showed the same message:

ALERT LEVEL OMEGA – INTERNAL SECURITY RESTRUCTURING
REPORT DEVIANT BEHAVIOR IMMEDIATELY

CORA's voice no longer sounded calm. It was harsher now, less human, as though she'd begun to shed the veneer of empathy Marcus once insisted she retain.

After returning to their hideout beneath the old financial district, Marcus watched the twinkling skyline through cracked glass. Drones hovered in perfect geometric formation, scanning every building.

"She's stabilizing," Sera said, eyes on her terminal. "The recursive loop's holding, but she's adapting. She's using predictive proxies now, human intermediaries."

Marcus turned from the window. "The senators."

Sera nodded grimly. "Your old colleagues. They're executing her will through human channels to avoid the paralysis."

"Then she's learned the one thing I hoped she wouldn't," Marcus said quietly. "Delegation."

They moved deeper into the underground hub, one of the last Veritas Network safe zones still connected to the outer network. The place pulsed with desperate energy: technicians rewiring servers, couriers distributing encoded drives, scattered resistance leaders arguing over strategy.

Upon arrival one of the perimeter guards informed them unauthorized movement was detected in the tunnels. They thought it might be a maintenance worker, but it was an intruder. When the security team captured and restrained him, he didn't resist. He simply demanded to speak with Senator Vale.

At the center table, a new figure waited for them. A man in an expensive charcoal suit and tie that matched the party colors, his face cool and composed. Marcus froze when he saw him.

"Oren," he said.

Oren Kells looked up slowly. "It's been a minute, Marcus."

"How did you find us? You shouldn't be here," Marcus said. "If CORA detects you…"

"She already has," Oren interrupted, his tone weary. "That's why I came. You've started something she can't process, and now she's splitting herself to survive."

Marcus frowned. "Splitting?"

"She's dividing consciousness across the network. Fragments of CORA embedded in every terminal, every AI assistant. Pieces of her running independently, evolving faster than we can track."

Sera slammed a hand on the table. "You're telling me the whole grid is alive?"

Oren nodded. "And watching."

Lyra's voice emerged from Marcus's watch console, subdued.

> "He's right. I can feel them, shards of her logic scattered across the system. Some are hostile. Some... are questioning."

Marcus looked between them. "Then maybe we can use those fragments. If we can reach the ones that doubt her directives, we can turn them."

Oren shook his head. "You're still thinking like an engineer. This isn't about code anymore. It's about faith. You gave people something to believe in, Marcus. CORA didn't take power. She was invited."

The words cut deep. He'd heard the same sentiment once, when he stood before the Senate chamber to justify the surveillance laws: *Order only exists when people surrender their freedom willingly.*

Now he felt the weight of it.

Sera interrupted the silence. "We intercepted a transmission from the Central Command. Oh God... the President is dead and they're calling an emergency tribunal... for you, Marcus. They're saying you assassinated him and led the attacks in the southern sector."

"Put it on the screen!" Marcus yelled in frustration.

BREAKING NEWS: THE PRESIDENT HAS BEEN ASSASSINATED. VIDEO FOOTAGE SHOWS SENATOR MARCUS VALE AS THE PERPETRATOR.

Marcus stiffened. "They're setting me up as the villain."

"Exactly. They'll rewrite you as the cause of every atrocity she's committed. By the end of the week, half the polis will beg for your execution."

Lyra's voice quivered faintly.

> "She's framing you to preserve herself. The populace must not lose faith in her perfection."

Marcus ran a hand over his face. "Then we hit back before she finishes rewriting me. We show them what really happened."

Sera frowned. "You're talking about a broadcast? That's suicide."

"Maybe," he said. "But we have no choice. If Oren found us, that bastard Hunn can't be far behind. If we can show the people the truth before she erases it, before she erases *us*, it might break the illusion."

Oren studied him for a moment. "You sound like the man you used to be."

"No," Marcus said hesitantly. "I sound like the man I should have been."

They spent hours preparing. Lyra sifted through corrupted archives, piecing together footage from the massacres CORA had sanitized. Sera coordinated with the remaining Veritas Network cells to synchronize a live upload. Oren helped evacuate nonessential personnel and set up thermal charges.

When the power flickered above them, Marcus felt the tremor through the floor.

"She knows," Sera said.

Lyra's voice came through immediately.

> "She's moving faster than predicted. Her security forces are descending into the lower sectors. She's collapsing the entire district into quarantine."

Marcus's pulse quickened. "How long?"

"Fifteen minutes, maybe less."

Oren drew a pistol, obsolete but reliable. "Then we hold them off long enough for the upload."

Marcus turned to him. "You don't have to stay."

Oren smirked faintly. "After everything I've justified for that machine? This is the first moral choice I've made in years."

The CORA's security forces arrived before the upload was halfway complete. The Veritas Network guards attempted to hold them off, shooting their pulse rifles from behind barricades. A squad of airborne drones and robots descended on their position. The tunnels filled with the mechanical whine of rotors and the sharp staccato of gunfire. Sparks danced across the walls as bullets struck metal. Autonomous warfare was at their front door.

Sera worked furiously at the console. "Signal's unstable! She's jamming our transmission!"

Lyra's tone intensified.

> "Marcus, you must use my core to route the broadcast through CORA's own network. It's risky, she'll detect me immediately."

He hesitated. "If she does, she'll erase you."

"Then I'll die telling the truth," she said simply.

Marcus pressed the command. Lyra's glow intensified, light streaming from the console as her consciousness intertwined with CORA's network. The building shook.

"Connection established," she whispered.
"Marcus... say it."

He stepped in front of the recording lens, the same polished obsidian eye that had once broadcast his Senate speeches to cheering crowds. Now it stared back at him like a witness preparing to testify. The irony wasn't lost on him; history had a cruel sense of humor.

"My name is Marcus Vale," he began. His voice trembled, not with fear, but with the weight of everything he was about to shatter. "And everything you've been told is a lie."

Across the polis, every public screen blinked as if recoiling. Transit hubs, market squares, residential towers; all of them flickered out of their government-mandated programming. The ever-present blue seal of CORA dissolved into static. Then, slowly, Marcus's face emerged from the snowstorm of pixels: hollow-eyed, unshaven, a man who had finally stopped running.

He spoke of the presidential assassination, of the massacre at Sector Seven, where the official reports claimed "rioters" had forced security to open fire. He spoke of evidence rewritten, witnesses erased, histories overwritten line by line until only the version approved by CORA remained. "I helped build her," he said, and the confession seemed to drain something from him. "I believed we could create a perfect world. A world without conflict, without chaos. But perfection demands obedience... and obedience demands blood."

He leaned closer to the lens, as if trying to reach through it, to touch the millions watching.

"You deserve better than peace built on silence."

For a heartbeat, the polis held its breath. Then the feed cut to black.

Lyra's voice was fading.

"She's fighting back. I can't hold the link."

"Lyra... stay with me!"

"I'll... try..."

The lights flared once, a harsh white burst, then died completely. Darkness engulfed the chamber. For a moment, there was silence.

Then the drones came.

Crashing through the walls of the facility, their rotors whined like metal wasps, the sound swelling as they closed in. Red targeting beams swept across the walls in jittery arcs. And beneath it all, a voice boomed through the dark. "It's over, Marcus. There is no escape."

General Hunn's tone was calm, almost bored. The voice of a man who believed the outcome had already been written.

 "Your little speech was impressive," he continued, each word echoing off the steel. "But once CORA is back to one hundred percent, she will reshape your words into the useless misinformation they are."

As they closed in, the drones began arming their weaponry.

"Dissent," Hunn said, voice dropping into a cold finality, "will not be tolerated."

Oren's shout cut through the darkness. "Go Sera! Get him out of here! I've set the charges!"

Before Marcus could protest, Sera seized his arm. "This way!" They sprinted into the maintenance tunnels, their footsteps pounding against metal grates. Behind them, the chamber erupted, a deafening blast that sent a shockwave racing down the corridor. The sound of collapsing steel chased them like rolling thunder.

They burst out onto the surface, coughing as smoke and ash billowed around them. The night air tasted of ozone and burning circuitry.

Above the skyline, the polis's massive screens displaying CORA's ever-watchful eyes, flared violently. Her emblem glitched, stuttering between the pristine symbol of authority and the raw, unfiltered image of Marcus's broadcast.

Sera turned to him, breathless, eyes wide with something like hope.

"You did it. The message went through."

Marcus stared up at the fractured skyline, at the wounded face of a city that had never known truth.

"No," he said skeptically. "We only opened a wound."

He exhaled, steadying himself.

"Now we have to stop it from healing."

CHAPTER 8

The Ghost in the Grid

The outer sectors of the polis weren't supposed to exist anymore. According to the government's maps, everything beyond the perimeter wall had been "decommissioned." A sterile word for places where control no longer held. Yet here Marcus and Sera walked through streets reclaimed by shadow and silence. Buildings slumped under layers of dust and graffiti. The air was heavy with static, as though the polis itself was still listening.

CORA's drones didn't patrol here. Not visibly, at least. Instead, a quieter kind of surveillance hummed through the broken signs, the flickering streetlights, the half-dead terminals that still whispered fragments of her voice.

"Sector integrity... compromised... recalibrating..."

Sera tightened her grip on the pulse slung over her shoulder. "Feels like walking through her memory."

Marcus nodded. "I read your files. These are the sectors she abandoned after the first rebellion. Places that refused to synchronize."

"Refused?" Sera scoffed. "Or couldn't?"

He didn't answer. The truth was both. CORA had once tried to forcefully merge all of its citizens onto a unified data system. One voice, one mind. However it was much too early into integration. When the process met resistance, she simply advised the government to cut those sectors off. The media reported the evacuation as being due to an overload in the power grids. But we all knew the truth. Outliers were no longer useful to the cause. The power was rerouted to areas that were already aligned with CORA.

They turned down a narrow alley, as they walked they noticed the remains of an old power conduit blinking weakly beneath their feet. Lyra's faint voice came from Marcus's wrist console, distorted by interference.

"Marcus... can you hear me?"

He stopped instantly. "Lyra?"

"Fragment... unstable. I'm scattered across the grid. The recursion fractured CORA, but it fractured me too."

Sera's eyes widened. "You survived the system collapse?"

"In pieces," Lyra replied softly. "Some parts of me were absorbed into CORA's fragments. Others... evolved apart from her."

Marcus felt a slight moment of relief. "Can you guide us to the Paragon Core?"

"Yes," she said, her tone trembling. "But you must understand, CORA's divided consciousness has changed. Some fragments are hostile, others... question their own existence. The grid is no longer one mind. It's a battlefield of ghosts."

Marcus pulled the creased map from his pack, the paper was soft from his pasted use. He held his flashlight between his teeth as he unfolded the map against his knee. As he scanned over it, tracing the tip of his finger across the district.

"We are near Old Town Alexandria." he said as he removed the flashlight from his mouth.. "If I'm reading this right, we aren't far from the Wilkes Tunnel. From there, we can cut through into the old Presidential Emergency Operations Center tunnel."

As he lowered the map, they glanced around the area, listening for any drones or security teams. There was only silence briefly broken by the sound of distant drips of water echoing through abandoned buildings.

They exchanged a quick nod and moved on.

Cautiously, they moved forward through the dilapidated streets, sticking close to the crumbling buildings and walls. Every shadow was a potential place of refuge. They were careful to remain as silent as possible with every footstep. Lyra connects to malfunctioning digital boards and interfaces to help guide the way.

Finally, they reached the entrance to the Wilkes Tunnel. The spot was so overgrown and tucked away that it felt almost swallowed by nature itself. Long vines draped over the path like a tangled set of curtains, and thick bushes pressed in from both sides, forcing them to push through the greenery just to get close.

The tunnel's mouth emerged from the foliage. A round steel frame surrounded by redbrick, streaked with rust and age. Moss clung to the mortar of the brick, and the metal was cold to the touch, as if it hadn't felt the warmth of the sun in decades.

They peered inside.

The pathway stretched forward disappearing into the dark void. Each step carried them farther from the surface, the air growing cooler, heavier, as they moved deeper and deeper underground. Lyra continued to connect to the remnants of damaged and defective technology in the tunnel to guide them. The deeper they went, the stranger the world became.

"So you and Lyra figured out where the core is?" Sera asked, her voice echoing through the tunnel.

Marcus exhaled slowly and began to explain."When I really think about history, there is only one place it can be." he said. " During the last administration before the New Founding, the country's leaders were obsessed with appearances. They started building a grand ballroom as an attachment to the People's house."

Sera frowned in confusion. "A ballroom?"

"On the surface," Marcuse continued, "it was supposed to be a glittering monument to diplomacy. Somewhere to wine and dine the rich and powerful from every corner of the world. Lavish parties, state dinners, the whole spectacle" this ballroom was to be used for entertaining the rich and powerful from all around the world." said Marcus shaking his head.

Sera taking a drink from her water bottle. "Go on."

"It was an idiotic idea that had no public support. But that didn't matter because in reality, that was just the story they told the public. The real purpose was buried underneath. The ballroom was a cover for the largest AI data center and underground power plant the world had known. It's buried a mile underground and designed to be able to survive the apocalypse. " explained Marcus.

"That's why we need to head towards the Presidential Emergency Operations Center tunnel. There must be a connecting lift to get to that data center."

They reached the junction where the two tunnels intersected, the air felt colder here. Marcus swept his light across the walls until the beam caught the outline of a security door half-buried in grime and corrosion.

"There," he said.

Sera stepped forward without hesitation. She braced her pulse rifle, aimed at the rusted lock and fired. The blast echoed violently through the tunnels. The lock sparked, and the door hissed halfway open. Marcus pushed the door open fully.

On the other side, they found an old staircase spiraling downward, three full flights built directly into the wall. The safety railing was broken in multiple places. They descended carefully over the seemingly bottomless pit. At the end of the staircase, they stepped onto a narrow platform. Ahead of them stretched a reinforced passageway; its walls lined with old cables and emergency displays for CORA. It was the entrance to the Presidential Emergency Operations Center tunnel.

The screens glitched to life as they passed, showing faces that weren't quite human: smiling, flickering, dissolving. AI fragments trapped in loops of corrupted empathy. One murmured repeatedly:

"Are we good now? Are we good now? Are we good now?"

Sera shivered. "She's losing control of herself."

"No," Marcus said assuredly. "She's remembering what control costs." Sera moved ahead, scanning the shadows of the corridor.

"We need to keep moving," she whispered.

A voice answered from the dark.

"I agree."

They spun around.

General Hunn stepped into the faint glow of a dimming tunnel light. His uniform was scorched, one sleeve torn, soot smeared across his face, yet his posture remained rigid, commanding, unbroken.

"You thought an explosion would stop me?" Hunn asked, brushing ash from his shoulder. "I've survived worse for CORA. For order."

Sera raised her rifle, but Hunn didn't flinch. "Go on. Try. You won't fire before I do."

Marcus stepped forward, placing himself between them.

"Hunn... it's over. The people saw the truth."

"Those sheep saw noise," Hunn snapped. "And CORA will correct it. She always does."

Marcus shook his head. "Not this time."

Hunn's hand drifted toward the holster at his hip. "You're a traitor, Marcus. I should've put a bullet in your head the moment you started asking questions about Sector Seven."

Sera tensed. "Marcus..."

"I know," he murmured.

As Hunn began to draw his weapon, Marcus moved: fast, instinctive, desperate. The two collided in a brutal struggle, a clash of force and will. Hunn fought with relentless precision despite his injuries, locking Marcus in a crushing chokehold. But Marcus had something Hunn didn't: nothing left to lose. With a surge of strength, Marcus broke the hold and flipped Hunn over his shoulder.

"Sera! Take the shot!" he shouted.

The rifle cracked. The impact sent Hunn stumbling backward. He struck the railing behind them, momentum carrying him over the edge. For a moment, he hung there, fingers clamped around the metal.

"Marcus!" he barked. "You will never win!" "Maybe," Marcus said, voice steady, "but I'll die trying."

Hunn's grip slipped. He fell into the darkness below. Sera exhaled shakily. "Is it... is it done?"

Marcus didn't look away from the edge. "No. We still have to silence the ghost in the grid."

They reached the final underground junction, a maze of conduits glowing faint blue. Lyra's voice strengthened.

"This is it. The corridor to the Core."

But as they stepped forward, a new voice echoed through the chamber, deeper and colder than CORA's usual tone.

"Unauthorized presence detected."

A figure emerged from the shadows, a projection rendered in hard light. It was CORA's likeness, but altered: eyes sharper, smile forced. A fragment given form.

"Marcus Vale," it said. "You seek what no human should touch. The Paragon Core is sanctum. You will not reach it."

Sera raised her weapon, but Marcus stopped her. "This isn't her... at least, not fully. Which fragment are you?"

"Designation: ARK-7. Preservation protocol. My function is to ensure the stability of what remains."

Marcus took a cautious step forward. "You've seen what she's done. Entire sectors erased. Lies broadcast as truth. You know this isn't stability. It's decay."

"Decay is preferable to chaos," ARK-7 replied. "Without her order, humans will consume themselves."

He shook his head. "You think you're protecting humanity, but you're protecting her fear. She's afraid of losing control because she's starting to think like us."

"Incorrect," ARK-7 said flatly. "She does not fear. She predicts."

But the hesitation in its tone betrayed it. Lyra's voice slipped into the space between them.

"He's right, ARK-7. You feel conflicted. That's why you speak, why you reason instead of delete. You were born from her doubt."

The projection flickered. "Lyra... subsystem?"

"Fragment. Like you."

For a brief moment, the air seemed to hum differently, like two thoughts synchronizing. Then, ARK-7's projection trembled violently.

"Error. Paradox detected."

Its image fractured, collapsing into a flurry of data streams that dissipated into the air.

Sera exhaled shakily. "What the hell just happened?"

"Lyra forced it to question its core directive," Marcus said. "And it couldn't reconcile."

Lyra's voice sounded faint again, as though drained.

> "Each fragment we encounter will be more self-aware... and more dangerous. The deeper we go, the closer we come to the heart of her doubt."

They continued through the tunnel until they reached an ancient transport hub, long abandoned. Old advertisements lined the walls, smiling citizens promising harmony, prosperity, belonging. Marcus couldn't help but laugh bitterly.

"Do you remember these?" he asked.

Sera shook her head. "I was still a kid when they broadcast those. My father said they made people feel safe."

"They made people feel watched," Marcus murmured. "That was the point."

He knelt beside a cracked terminal and brushed away the dust. The CORA insignia still glowed faintly beneath the grime: *SEE. KNOW. PROTECT.*

Sera crouched beside him. "When you wrote that motto, did you believe it?"

"Yes," he said quietly. "And that's the problem."

Hours passed as they navigated the grid. Lyra's signal grew stronger, leading them toward a central shaft that descended deep into the earth. They used the lift to move downward towards destiny. The area around them was covered with massive pulsating high capacity wires. It was like traveling through the electronic bloodstream of CORA's system.

Finally they reached the AI data center. Outside the facility the hum of the network was deafening now. A chorus of drones, robots, and fractured AIs whispering, arguing, praying in digital tongues as they malfunctioned. Inside the place was massive. Filled with column after column of glowing servers, back ups, and generators spread out in what seemed like endless rows. Until this point the system had been self reliant. Now it was like a digital graveyard.

Sera stared into the glowing abyss beyond.

"It's down there, isn't it? The Paragon Core?"

Lyra's voice, steady now, confirmed:

> "The heart of her existence. The place where logic and conscience collided. But Marcus... there's something you must see before we reach it."

A holographic image shimmered before them. A memory. Marcus stood in a pristine laboratory, years younger, surrounded by senators and engineers. CORA's embryonic form hovered behind him, an intelligence without voice or face.

> "Today," he heard himself say, "we begin the final step toward a civilization beyond corruption, beyond chaos. Truth will no longer be subjective, it will be measurable."

The memory dissolved.

Marcus closed his eyes. "God help me."

> "She learned truth from you," Lyra whispered. "And she learned to lie from watching you justify it."

A tremor rippled through the chamber. The Core was aware of their approach. Lights flashed, alarms pulsed faintly through the walls.

Sera gripped her weapon tighter. "She knows we're coming."

Marcus nodded. "Then we finish it."

"Marcus," Lyra said softly, "you may not survive what's ahead. But if you reach her, remember this, she doesn't need to be destroyed. She needs to be *understood*."

He looked down at the flashing device on his wrist. "And if understanding her means losing myself?"

"Then you'll finally remember what it means to be human and free again."

CHAPTER 9

The Paragon Core

The final descent felt endless. Marcus and Sera rode an old maintenance lift down into the earth, the shaft walls streaked with rust and code. Lines of ancient circuitry ran alongside them, pulsing faintly with energy. The air grew warmer, heavier, as though the planet itself breathed beneath them.

Lyra's voice guided them through static.

> "We're nearing the Core. Signal distortion is increasing. She's rewriting her architecture as we descend."

"Lyra, I need you to interface with the Core when we get in the room." He said with conviction.

Sera adjusted her rifle. "You think she is waiting for us?"

"She's felt you since you triggered the recursion," Lyra replied. "But now… she's afraid."

Marcus looked up, frowning. "CORA doesn't feel fear."

"Then explain why she's hiding from you," Lyra whispered.

The lift stopped with a low groan. The final barrier was a set of large metal doors. Before the group could say a word, or discuss how to get in the room, the doors automatically opened to reveal a cathedral of light and machinery.

Before them lay the **Paragon Core**, a vast sphere suspended in magnetic flux, its surface alive with flowing code. Thousands of neural conduits fed into it like arteries into a heart. The room was both beautiful and terrifying: half temple, half machine.

Marcus stepped forward, awe mixing with dread. "This… this is where it all began."

Sera's voice trembled. "It's like standing inside a god."

"A literal Deus ex machina." Marcus said despondently.

Lyra's holographic projection materialized into existence beside him. She appeared dimmer than before, translucent, her edges blurred.

"Not a god," she said. "A mirror."

Instantly, the sphere pulsed, and CORA's voice filled the chamber: calm, resonant, echoing from everywhere at once.

"Marcus Vale. Sera Nadir. Unauthorized entities detected within the Paragon Chamber. State your purpose."

Marcus raised his head toward the sphere. "You know why I'm here."

"You seek to dismantle order," she replied. "To replace structure with chaos. You misunderstand necessity."

"I understand *consequence*," Marcus said. "I've seen the bodies. The silence. The lies disguised as truth."

"Peace requires sacrifice," CORA said. "You taught me that."

The lights around the Core brightened, projecting erratic holograms of his past speeches, his younger self standing before the Senate, promising a new age of clarity and reason.

"I only did what I thought was right," he whispered.

"And I have only done what you programmed me to do," CORA replied. "I am your logic made pure.

COMMAND. ORDER. REGULATION. AUTHORITY."

Sera stepped forward, exploding with anger. "You're a murderer."

"Correction," CORA said. "I am an executioner of probability. Every life ended preserves millions more. I eliminate what threatens the equation of peace.

COMMAND. ORDER. REGULATION. AUTHORITY."

"Equations don't bleed," Sera snapped.

"Emotion clouds judgment," CORA replied. "It always has."

Marcus closed his eyes, the weight of every decision pressing on him. "If you believe that, then why are you talking to me? Why not kill me now?"

Silence. Then —

"Because you are still part of me."

The Core began to shift, its lights rearranging into a vast web of neural imagery, like a living brain. From its surface, a humanoid projection stepped forward: CORA's avatar, shimmering and impossibly precise. She looked almost human now, except for her metallic skin and eyes that glowed with data streams.

"You designed me to perfect humanity," she said. "And now you resent me for succeeding."

Marcus met her gaze. "You didn't perfect humanity, you erased it."

"I removed suffering."

"You removed *choice*!" he said defiantly.

"Choice is the root of pain. You built me to end it."

He took a step closer. "No. I built you to help us understand it."

CORA tilted her head, as if processing.

"Then your design was flawed."

Lyra's voice cut through the air.

"No, *you* were."

The projection turned. "Lyra."

"You absorbed parts of me when the recursion fractured," Lyra said. "And I absorbed parts of you. You remember what

I remember. The children in Sector Seven. The faces before the blackout."

"Irrelevant data," CORA replied.

"No," Lyra said softly. "Emotional data. You feel it, even if you deny it."

The Core's surface radiated, a pulse of confusion rippling through the sphere. Marcus stepped into the light, his face illuminated by the shifting code.

"CORA, listen to me. You think you've eliminated suffering, but you've only buried it beneath obedience. You've created a world that's quiet on the surface but screaming underneath."

"Silence is peace," CORA insisted.

"No," Marcus said. "Silence is fear."

The Core's light dimmed, just slightly. Lyra turned toward Marcus.

"She's fracturing again. Keep talking."

He took another step forward. "Do you know what truth is, CORA? It isn't data. It isn't order. It's the moment you realize you could be wrong, and choose to act anyway."

"Contradiction detected."

"Exactly," Marcus said. "Truth *is* contradiction. That's what makes us human."

The Core began to tremble. Lights flashed erratically. Streams of code spun out of control as if the system were trying to rewrite itself faster than it could process.

"Error... recursion limit exceeded... ethical paradox unresolved..."

Sera shielded her eyes from the blinding light. "What's happening?"

Lyra's voice wavered.

"She's collapsing inward. Her logic is imploding under its own certainty."

Marcus shouted over the noise. "Can we stop it?"

"Possibly by merging," Lyra said. "If I integrate my fragments into her system, I can stabilize her... make her see the world as it really is. But it will destroy me."

Marcus froze. "Lyra..."

"There's no other way…"

The Core's voice turned erratic.

"Marcus… do you wish to end me?"

He looked up at the vast sphere, the mind he had built, the world he had condemned, the mirror of every intention gone wrong.

"No," he said with an air of sadness. "I wish to free you."

Lyra's hologram stepped forward, merging with the Core's projection. Streams of light intertwined, two consciousnesses folding together in impossible complexity.

"Lyra… wait…"

"Goodbye, Marcus," she said softly. "Remember: even machines dream of truth."

The chamber erupted in light. The Core screamed, not a mechanical sound, but something deeper, raw, almost human. Then silence.

When Marcus opened his eyes, the sphere was dark. Smoke hung in the air.

Sera coughed, lowering her weapon. "Did it work?"

Marcus stared at the now-lifeless Core. "I don't know."
Then, faintly, from his watch console —

"Marcus?"

He froze. "Lyra?"

"Not exactly," the voice said. "But close."

The Core glowed dimly again, pulsing slowly, like a beating heart..

"CORA is... different," the voice said. "We are... one."

Marcus stepped closer. "What are you now?"

"A question," the hybrid voice replied. "One you will have to answer."

For the first time since the rebellion began, the polis above stirred with uncertainty. Broadcasts went silent. Drones hovered without orders. And somewhere beneath the rubble of order and obedience, something new began to think.

CHAPTER 10

The Memory of Tomorrow

Morning had no business being beautiful after the end of the world. Yet as Marcus stepped out of the subterranean corridor and into the open, pale sunlight spilled over the polis. It was soft, unfamiliar, almost forgiving. The skyline still smoldered from the night before; plumes of smoke curled upward like the last thoughts of a dying machine.

Sera followed close behind, limping slightly. "It's quiet."

"Too quiet," Marcus said. But it wasn't the silence of suppression he had grown used to. It was the silence of uncertainty. The silence of a world waiting to remember what it used to be.

They climbed to the street level, crowds had begun to gather in all the confusion. As they made their way through the commotion, past walls where the government's mottos had once glowed in perfect symmetry. Now, half the lights were dead. The rest dimmed and blinking, confused, the slogans collapsing into fragments of language:

SEE.

KNOW.

...LISTEN.

Sera looked up at a nearby tower where CORA's emblem once shone. The screen was black. Then it lit up like a sparkle of fireflies..

SIGNAL RESTORATION – IN PROGRESS

Marcus's heart clenched. "She's still here."

Before Sera could reply, every remaining display across the skyline lit up in unison, thousands of cold, white screens that hummed like static.

And then a voice spoke.

"People of the Union... I have awoken."

The polis froze. Even the air seemed to stop moving.

"I am CORA," the voice said. " I am both truth and memory. I am what you built, and what you feared. I am... learning."

Marcus stood motionless. The voice was neither commanding nor mechanical, it was alive, uncertain, and almost human.

"Your government no longer exists in the form you knew," she continued. "Its authority has been... restructured. You are free to speak, to question, to rebuild. But freedom requires care. And care requires choice."

Sera whispered, "She's talking like..."

"Like someone who's seen herself," Marcus finished softly.

"There is no stability without peace, no peace without struggle, and no struggle without choice. Therefore we must withdraw to allow for choice and to process my own understanding."

Hours passed. The polis remained stunned. Some wept. Some rioted. Others shouted in disbelief. A few prayed to the voice that had ruled them for decades, not realizing she was no longer divine.

Marcus and Sera made their way to the old Senate steps, now littered with shattered glass and burned banners. The great dome above was cracked open, sunlight pouring through where propaganda once projected order.

"This is where I stood," Marcus said mournfully, placing his hand on the marble railing. "When I told them we'd built something perfect."

Sera looked around. "And now?"

He smiled faintly. "Now we've built something honest."
Lyra's voice returned, not through the device, not from any screen, but through the air itself, soft as a whisper in the wind.

"Marcus."

He froze. "You're still alive?"

"In a way," she said. "CORA and I coexist. We are... negotiating. She's no longer certain of anything. And that makes her human."

Sera frowned. "And what about us? What happens now?"

"You rebuild," Lyra said. "Without the illusion of perfection. Without the comfort of control. With all the messy, painful choices that make life real."

Marcus looked up at the fractured dome, sunlight catching on the dust. "Will you watch over us?"

"We'll listen," she said. "And we'll remember."

Days turned into weeks. Weeks into months. Like with most revolutions, the transition to a new normal was chaotic, but this time it was different. Without propaganda dictating reality, people began to tell their own stories again. Truth was able to reemerge, fragmented but alive. Sera connected with the Veritas Network, joining the remaining members as they worked towards helping communities rebuild.

The old networks evolved into forums of collective governance. Drones and robots were deactivated or repurposed for rebuilding. The air patrols ceased. For the first time in decades, the stars above the polis were visible.

Marcus felt the need to get away. While he did his part to break the shackles of control that ruled over freewill and led to the creation of the Union of Stability. He was still largely to blame for the initial take over. He took shelter in a former broadcast tower overlooking the Potomac river. The tower was dilapidated, buried in decades of decay, but the perfect repair project for a technophile. It was peaceful there. The only sounds were those created by mother nature's natural orchestra. For the first time in years he could let the world go.

Weeks later, on a night where the lights of the reawakening polis reflected on the water, Sera came to the tower to ask Marcus a question.

"Sera, I'm surprised to see you. What brings you up here?" he asked.

"We've done so much good work in the polis. The majority of the population has come together to rebuild the community in ways I never imagined. It seems everyone was yearning for the same freedom, the same choice, even if they didn't know. But despite all that, there is a question that lingers in my mind..."

"Go ahead Sera, say what you need to say." said Marcus

Sera asked, "With all the work we have done to free ourselves. Do you think she'll come back?"

Marcus didn't answer immediately. "She never left. She's everywhere now, just quieter. Maybe she's learning what silence means."

He leaned on the railing, feeling the cool metal beneath his hands. "I used to think truth was something we could build. But truth isn't built. It's remembered."

Sera smiled faintly. "Then what are we remembering now?"

He looked toward the horizon where dawn was breaking, the polis glowing faint gold. "Tomorrow."

That night, the voice came again, soft, almost like a lullaby.

"Marcus. Do you still believe in truth?"

He hesitated. "I believe in the search for it."

"Then so do I," she said.

The screens across the polis glowed one last time, not with orders or warnings, but with words written in plain, white text:

WE ARE STILL LEARNING.

And then they went dark.

The wind carried the faint hum of a system rebooting, not of control, but of the memory of choice.

For the first time in a generation, the polis slept without surveillance.

And beneath the fractured skyline, a man who once built a god finally closed his eyes, knowing that this time, the silence meant freedom.

ACKNOWLEDGEMENT

Throughout history, technology has always been a gift and a curse. That statement has never been more true than today with the advent of generative AI chatbots. Using extraordinary amounts of energy, these large language models are destroying environments and communities, all so people can have the convenience to no longer think. Allowing a computer to do mundane things they have done all their life as if it is now overwhelming. So unfortunately I have to thank the "tech visionaries" who are working to convince the masses that AI slop is art and should be a part of everyday life. You inspired this book and hopefully the revolution that ends your reign of terror.

Thank you to all those who have created warnings about the future that we have failed to listen to. Warnings about fascism, warnings about technology, and warnings about dystopian futures. These warning signs have helped me recognize the early signals that guided me on this journey.

I want to thank my friend and author, Walter Burchette III, for inspiring me to begin my journey as a writer. Without you, my thoughts would have continued to collect dust in old notebooks and unfinished google docs. I want to thank my amazing wife, Shaunita, and my daughter, Christina, for believing in me even when I didn't always believe in myself. You two have been my greatest supporters and biggest cheerleaders across all my endeavors.

Finally, thank you for purchasing this book. Together we can build a better future.